To Alex ~

Let your stories be told ~

from all your friends from
FoxFire Farm ~

Lowell Davis

JULY
1992

The Book on Chickens

the Book on Chickens

Written, Illustrated and Lived by Lowell Dav

PELICAN PUBLISHING COMPANY

Gretna 1992

Library of Congress Cataloging-in-Publication Data

Davis, Lowell.
    The book on chickens / written, illustrated, and lived by Lowell
Davis.
      p. cm.
    ISBN 0-88289-891-4. — ISBN 0-88289-890-6 (pbk.)
    1. Chickens—Humor. I. Title.
PN6231.C29D38 1992
741.5'973—dc20   91-23115
                                                 CIP

Manufactured in Hong Kong

Published by Pelican Publishing Company, Inc.
1101 Monroe Street, Gretna, Louisiana 70053

To my dad, who as a farmer didn't fully understand a career in art. But still he encouraged me. In fact, the reason I drew so much as a kid was I found that as long as I was drawing I didn't have to do chores.

The Book on Chickens

Far from the big cities, snugged in the foothills of the Ozark Mountains, is a farm_ a real farm. And on this farm is where Mr. Lowell and his family lives. It was a cold, February winter morning as Mr. Lowell made his way to the chicken house.

Dawn was just breaking a̶ peeping through the w̶ in the chicken ho̶

It must Betty. at I'd say

Just a̶ getting ready to put his w̶ Clara jumped off her perch w̶ ment. "Look at those windows! Jack̶ did a number on them.

"I'd say it got to ten below," said Nell.

THE FAR SIDE

Chicken sexual fantasies

A sudden gust of wind disturbed the late awakening chickens as Mr. Lowell's image appeared in the doorway...

"Only one egg today ⟶ are you girls trying to set a Guinness Book of World Records for the least number of eggs that 14 hens can lay in one day? Not even enough for breakfast!"

"He'd complain if someone was goin' to hang him with a new rope."

"I don't know what he expects. My pipes have been frozen up since November."

Honey your pipes have been frozen up since....."

Cabin fever had really set in — Winter was taking its toll.
Tempers were short, so the days were made up of small talk,
gossip and a lot of arguing.

Days seemed like weeks... weeks like months
and months like years.

Everyone was thinking that spring would never arrive.

Finally one morning the sweet sound of a robin's song drifted through the window. Nell was the first to hear the sound and gave the alarm ———————— "Spring is here!"

Big Jack was off the roost in a flash . . . he ran over and threw up the sash.

"Holy Moly it's spring," and he stepped outside.

"Come on out girls. Spring has sprung
thar's bugs to be chased and worms
to be a-diggin'"

Clara was next to make her appearance.

Big Jack was already up to his old antics...
   chasing spring's first moths and feeling like a real spring chicken.

It wasn't long before all the hens were busy dusting and soaking up the warm sun. How good it felt after a cold winter cooped up in the chicken house. While the other hens were doing their thing, Goldie and Clara went for a stroll around the farm.

In fact, this was Goldie's first spring on the farm. She had just hatched on the 8th of July of last year.

"Well, I declare, look Goldie daffodils. That's my favorite flower. I don't know if it's 'cause they're so purty or just because they're the first flowers of spring."

"Yes, they are quite beautiful," said Goldie. "But what I want to know is, where are all those available roosters that were on the farm last fall?"

"Well Dearie, ya know ole Big Jack's de·cock·o·de·walk around this farm and the chicken house is his territory. So the other roosters spend the winter in the barn and the corn crib."

Well that's a relief," said Goldie.
"I was afraid Big Jack was the only eligible bachelor around. Of course, there ain't nothin' wrong with him he is terribly handsome ya' know."

"Come on Goldie we'd better be headin' back to the chicken yard or ole Big Jack will be comin' lookin' fer us. He'll swear that you've been seein' Willy the Wyandotte who hangs out around the buggy shed. Don't think I haven't noticed that Big Jack is moonstruck over you."

Mr. Lowell came out and opened all the windows
so that the fresh breeze could blow through the chicken house.

Kerchooo?
oops!

Spring was in the air and with spring there was
romance in the hearts of everyone on the farm.

The nights grew warmer and
Big Jack's heart grew fonder.

He finally edged himself so he
could roost near Goldie...
while the other hens were dreaming of barn roosters.

One morning Big Jack had just headed out the door when Dr. Stanley, the hen house mouse doctor, says to him, "Hey Big Jack, from the 'for what it's worth department' — I hear through the grape-vine that Willy the Wyandotte is goin' to make his big play for your heartthrob today, ya' know ——— Goldie.

And somethin' else Jack — you've been lookin' a little green around the gills lately. Maybe you should come in for a checkup tomorrow."

Later on that day... .

"Yoo Hoo, Goldie baby, anytime you want a real man, you know where I hang out. I wouldn't mind sportin' you around this farm any time."

"Well I declare, look what kind of riff-raff will come in if someone forgets to shut the gate."

"You ain't goin' to take that sittin' down, are you Big Jack?"

Well, this really got ole Big Jack's hackles up and his comb got
redder and redder.
"This is the last straw," he says to himself. "I'm just goin'
to have to teach this Romeo a quick lesson in some manners."

It was when Willy saw the glistening of Big Jack's spurs
——he started having some second thoughts about this situation.

He started to back out through the gate,
but it was too late.

With Big Jack in hot
pursuit——through
the barnyard they went.

Into the orchard, then by the
old pump where Willy slipped
on some loose gravel as he turned
the corner near the chicken yard.

All the commotion woke up Hayseed the tomcat who
had been snoozing in the sun.

Willy was really embarrassed, especially in front of all of those hens. He had turned chicken and even lost a fight —— all within a few humiliating minutes.

Willy headed home with his tail tucked between his legs.

Big Jack proudly strode back past the girls without even a feather out of place.

"Oh Goldie, he is such a male chauvinist, ain't he?"

"Well, I'm kinda old fashioned I guess, I call it valiant."

By this time Big Jack had worked up a powerful appetite. As he was enjoying his chicken scratch, he noticed the old chicken house that his grandfather had been hatched in. It had been deserted for years, but all spring he'd seen Mr. Lowell working and fixing it up —— going in and spending most of the day.

Curiosity had finally gotten the best of him, and now that Willy the Wyandotte wasn't a threat to his territory, he decided it was time to go and check it out...

The door was left open ——.
Big Jack peeped in.

"Holy Moly," exclaimed Jack.

"So this is what Mr. Lowell spends his days a-doin'."

Upon realizing that no one was in this strange lookin' chicken house, and that there were no other roosters in there ——— he decided to venture inside.

"Wow!" Jack exclaimed. "I've been to two county fairs, a cake walk and a dog fight, and I ain't never seen the likes of this before."

Then, lo and behold there it was —— bigger than Dallas —— a painting of Big Jack in all his glory.

Big Jack decided to take it and hang it in the chicken house, hoping that maybe Goldie would see it and be impressed.

—And that's the way he decided to propose to her.

No sooner had he hung it on an old nail when Mr. Lowell came in.

"It didn't take any Sherlock Holmes to figure out who took that picture out of my studio Big Jack. Your muddy footprints led me here. Now, you know what the Good Book says about taking things that don't belong to you.

You may keep it this time, but from now on, ask first.

You are welcome in my studio any time . . . but next time wipe your feet."

Big Jack went back outside into the chicken yard, feeling pretty guilty . . . but this only lasted for a minute.

His mind soon went back to Goldie. What could he get her for a wedding ring (in case she accepted his proposal)?

He thought to himself, maybe binder twine, but no, that wouldn't last and he certainly wanted something that would last.

Well, I guess I could find some baling wire, that would last.

No! That would be ugly, an old piece of wire for a ring.

I know," exclaimed Big Jack, "I'll go and ask Stanley, the chicken house doctor. He's got all the answers."

Dr. Stanley, the chicken house mouse, was sitting there in the feed bin enjoying the silence. The hen party had just left and Betty's shrill voice was still ringing in his ears.

And that Nell, always talking about her home remedies, and Deloris complaining about her rheumatism — and that she always needed her daily Roop remedy — which is about 90 proof.

And then there was Edna, her beak always a-flappin'. No wonder she was still an old maid.

So now, as he was just resting his ears, he heard sounds at the chicken house front door...

It was Big Jack's spurs clicking together as he walked.

At that moment the door to the feed bin flew open.
Big Jack's silhouette appeared in the doorway as he
waited for his eyes to adjust to the darkness.

"Well Big Jack. I'm glad to see you took my advice and came in to see me. Your coloring hasn't looked good to me lately."

"On the contrary Doc. I've never felt better in my life. I didn't come in for a check-up. I wanta ask Goldie to marry me and I don't have a ring. Have you got any ideas...?"

"Well congratulations — though I can't say it takes me by surprise... I've heard all of that flowery talk and seen those goggle eyes that you've been making at her lately.

"Yes, I think I have just the ticket for you —

"Mr Lowell used these chicken rings years ago to mark the hens that were in the nest box. He would put one on the leg so he would know which one was laying.

"And they come in all different colors — red, blue, green — and I think I saw a yellow one in there somewhere."

"Oh Doc, you're not only a great doctor, you're a genius. Yellow, that's Goldie's favorite color. Can you find one?"

Dr. Stanley dug through the box of rings. Finally, near the bottom, he came up with one.

"Here Big Jack," he said. "I knew it was in there somewhere."

Big Jack took the ring, thanked the Doc kindly, and shut the door behind him as he went merrily on his way.

Big Jack went back to his portrait and straightened it. He had put it near the water fountain so Goldie would see it when she and the girls came in for a drink.

Now all Big Jack had to do was sit back and wait to see what Goldie's reaction would be. Then he had to get up enough nerve to pop the question.

He decided to just wait — so he hid behind the door.

In a very short time he heard Goldie and the girls coming in for their afternoon chat around the water fountain.

Betty was the first one in — so she was the first to see it.
"Heavens to Betsy — I wonder who hung this here, and just who it's for?"
Just about that time Goldie stepped up and saw the picture — her heart
nearly jumped out through her feathers.

"Oh, isn't he the most handsome
   rooster in the whole world," said Goldie.

"I would just love to have that painting...
   but I'd really rather have the real thing,
   Big Jack himself."

Big Jack could hardly contain himself when he heard Goldie's remarks. He was so excited he thought he'd come unglued. He decided to lay low until the girls had left the chicken house. Later, as he strolled out, he anticipated finding Goldie alone so he could pop the question. But then he went to the garden — his favorite spot. There he could build up his courage.

He kept a wary eye out for Mr. Lowell ——— who would surely chase him away.

Out of the corner of his eye Big Jack saw Goldie
all alone. She was standing there looking
into one of Miss Charlotte's flower beds.

This was his chance.

Goldie was saying to herself____
    "Iris, they're my favorite...Oh no, I
      think these tulips are. I don't know,
        maybe the grape hyacinths are my favorite—they're awfully pretty.

"No wait! I know, the most beautiful have to be these orange poppies__
      no maybe it's the_____"

Just then Big Jack stepped up behind her and said, "Goldie you're the prettiest flower of all."

Startled, Goldie turned around and said, "Oh Big Jack, I bet you say that to all the hens."

No, you're my only real heart throb, although I do look at the other hens, after all... I am a rooster, but you're the one I want to marry." The words just seemed to slip out.

"Marry you?" exclaimed Goldie. "Is this a proposal Jack?"

"Well ah...yes, I guess it is."

"Oh Jack! I can't think of anything I'd rather do than spend the rest of my life on this farm with you." And with that she gave him a peck on the cheek.

Big Jack was so excited that he wanted to go tell the world. He ran all over the farm telling the work horses; Blossom, the cow; Pearl and Butler, the sheep; the goats; Tom turkey; the gaggle of geese and Ozark Bell, the coon hound.

"Great!" Ozark said, "When's the big day?"

"Er, —— well, gosh, I don't know. I'll have to go ask Miss Goldie."

Big Jack went back to Goldie and asked her to set the date. She thought for a moment and then said, "May 15th —— that's my mother's birthday."

"May 15th?" exclaimed Big Jack. "But that's two weeks away. I was in hopes it would be tomorrow."

"There's too much to be done," said Goldie. "We've got to invite all our friends —— my wedding bonnet has to be made, and we'll have to ask Gus the gander if he will tie the knot."

The two weeks went by so slowly that it seemed like an eternity to Big Jack.

(No! No! Jack —— not until we're married!!!)

It was the day before the wedding and there was much excitement
due to the preparations _____ especially in the hen house.

That night it was hard for the critters on the farm to fall asleep ___
thinking about the exciting day tomorrow.

The Wedding Day

It was the biggest shindig that Foxfire Farm had ever seen!

They were all there: Edna, Clara, Neil, Betty and Della, who brought flowers. Blossom the cow and Durham the bull were there. Barney and Mike, the work horses, leaned over the fence —— so they were there. Hayseed the tomcat came out of the barnloft, so he was there too.

Garfield and Mary, the goats —— and their kids were there. Wilbur, the pig left his trough and was there.

And then there were Butler and Pearl the sheep —— they were there. Tom Turkey was there. Of course, the gaggle of geese were there.

And way in the background, even Willy the Wyandotte was there. All the barnyard roosters and hens were there.

Yes, they were all there.   There to see Big Jack and Goldie get hitched.

Lowell Davis

After all the I do's, and Mrs. Goldie throwin' her
bouquet of flowers to Edna, it was time for all the farm
animals to charivari * Big Jack and Goldie———
that's an old Missouri tradition.

Big Jack had to push Goldie around the farm in
a wheelbarrow so everyone could see
the bride's new ring.

Everyone was 'oing and 'ahing
over Goldie's ring and hollerin' to
Big Jack about what a beautiful spring bride he had——— but then, Jack
already knew that. The wheelbarrow ride ended up back at the chicken house
where Big Jack carried Goldie over the threshold.

* Charivari ——— that's what country folks do when someone gets married. They
sometimes throw the groom in the creek, and always make a lot of noise.

As they went in, they saw that Mr. Lowell had heard the news —
he had come out to the chicken house and painted Goldie's name
in front of her new nest box. Goldie was so proud, and happy too,
because it was right next to wise ol' Nell, who knew every remedy.

It was then that Big Jack decided that a hen house was no place for a
honeymoon — — not with all those gossipy old hens, ya' know.

The nights were warmer now
so Big Jack and Goldie moved
into the big walnut tree
just north of the chicken house.

He called it the Honeymoon Suite.

A couple of weeks after Big Jack and Goldie were roosting in the ole walnut tree, Goldie turned to Big Jack and said, "Honey, it's time, I think I'm going to lay my first egg."

"You're what? Going to lay your first egg? Here? Tonight?"

"No, no, honey — I think it will probably be tomorrow or the next day."

"Oh Goldie, that makes me so happy — I love you so much."

"Would you two love birds knock it off out there? We're tryin' to get some shut-eye!"

And they both closed their eyes and fell asleep.

The next day Goldie said to Big Jack, "I really don't want to hurt Mr. Lowell's feelings ——— since he painted my name on the nestbox, but I found a nice cool place under the corn crib where I've decided to lay my eggs ——— and that way...

Mr. Lowell won't have them for his breakfast."

So that very afternoon Goldie went under the corn crib ———. She told Jack to wait outside.

"Is that a cat under thar pa?"

"Hey Mom! What's for supper?"

"No ma, it's just some old chicken."

A short time later Goldie softly said, "Big Jack, you can come in now."

Lifting her wing she said, "There it is. What do you think?"

"Oh heartthrob——it's the most gorgeous egg that I've ever seen."

With that, he ran out and perched himself on a fence post and started crowing loudly and repeatedly. . .

Cock·a·doodle·do
Cock·a·doodle·do
Cock·a·doodl

Meanwhile _____ back in the henhouse . . .

Big Jack wanted to spend every minute of every day with Goldie. But once a day she would leave him and go under the corn crib to lay another egg.

Big Jack never seemed to know what to do with himself while Goldie was doing this. When she returned, he would always go to the nearest fencepost and crow as loud as he could.

One day Goldie went under the corn crib and Big Jack waited outside. He waited and he waited and he waited till the sun was setting over the hedgerow in the west pasture._____And still no Goldie.

By now it was getting the best of him. Jack went to the corncrib to see what was the matter.

"Goldie! Goldie, where are you?"

"Over here Jack, on my nest of eggs," replied Goldie.

"Well are you ever going to come out so that we can be together?" cried Jack.

"No, I'm sorry Jack", Goldie replied. "You will have to stay by yourself for awhile ___ till my eggs hatch."

"Well then", said Jack. "Will that be sometime tomorrow?"

"No, honey. It might be a long time. I've never hatched eggs before."

"You mean you might be there all day and night?"

"That's right dear," replied Goldie.

It was getting dark as Big Jack made his way back to the old walnut tree. He couldn't get any sleep that night because it was the loneliest night of his life.

The next day was no better. Big Jack just moped around like a lost pup. He even went back to the corncrib _____ but Goldie would have nothing to do with him. Then he went back to hang out around the hen house.

About that time Clara came out. She saw Big Jack and said, "Big Jack, you look awful! Maybe you should go see Dr. Stanley."

"No it's not that," Big Jack said. "I didn't get any sleep last night and Goldie is setting on her eggs. She's also in a real bad mood and she won't have anything to do with me _____. She thinks more of her eggs than she does of me. I don't think she loves me anymore."

"Oh no, she still loves you _____.
      She's what they call broody. That's when a hen is setting on a
      nest of eggs. She will only come out once a day to eat and
      get a drink of water... then she will go back to her eggs.
      But not to worry, it will only be for 21 days, Big Jack."

"Twenty-one days", Big Jack thought to himself, "it
      might as well be twenty-one years,"
      and with that he moped off.

Days went by and Big Jack just couldn't cheer himself up...then he saw Wren——Mr. Lowell's youngest daughter, headed for the privy.

He remembered what great sport it had been to chase her in his younger days, so when she came out he decided to chase her out of the chicken yard.

He just knew that would cheer him up.

Well, when Wren came out she saw him out of the corner of her eye, coming at her, full steam ahead. She took off running and just made it through the garden gate. Big Jack retreated and walked back to the chicken house not feeling any better than he had before.

Three long weeks had gone by.

Big Jack thought he would go back to the corncrib and check on Goldie.

This time she surprised him by saying, "Jack, come here. I want you to hear something."

"Hear what?" Big Jack asked as he entered.

"This peeping sound," cooed Goldie.

"You mean they've hatched?" shrilled Big Jack.

"No, no — not yet, maybe tomorrow," said Goldie. "They are still in the shells. But it's a sign that they are getting ready to hatch."

Big Jack was so happy as he came out from under the corn crib. That night he could hardly sleep again — thinkin' about what was going to happen tomorrow.

The next morning Big Jack crowed at the crack of dawn.

He couldn't wait to go back out to the corncrib.

He waited around till the warm morning sun
had lifted and its warmth had filled the air.

It was then that Goldie appeared with eight tiny
balls of fluff...

balls of yellow fluff that were darting about.

Needless to say, Big Jack was
so proud he was about to bust his
buttons———He wanted to take
Goldie and their peeps around the
farm and show them off.
    Well it was Spring, and there
were babies being born all over
the farm to other proud parents.

The first animals Goldie and
Big Jack wanted to show
their peeps to were
Butler and Pearl——the sheep.

"Hey, Butler——— what do you think
of our babies?" Big Jack asked proudly.
"Well, they're O.K. I guess——— but look at my own little lambie pies...
——they are much cuter."

Disappointed, Big Jack and Goldie made their way to see
Blossom, the cow. Blossom and her new
calf were grazing in the west pasture.

As Big Jack and Goldie, along with their peeps, approached ——— Jack asked Blossom what she thought of their cute babies.

Blossom said, "They are cute, but they don't compare to my baby Star."

Again, Big Jack and Goldie got the same answer from Garfield and Mary, the goats...

"Not as cute as our kids."

Well, by this time Big Jack and Goldie were really heartbroken.

It was getting late in the day, so they decided to go back and spend the evening under the corn crib.

On their way back they passed the gaggle of geese with their
newly hatched goslings.

The geese didn't even give the peeps a second look.
They had their noses snubbed so high in the air
that if it had been raining————————they would have drowned.

Big Jack and his family made it back to the corn crib just as the sun was
setting and they settled in for the night.

Summer nights — down on the farm

"Do white hens lay white eggs and brown hens lay brown ones?"

"They're white. Ain't that right Mom?"

"Yes, that's right. But don't say ain't."

"Daddy does."

[si]lly... it makes no difference [wha]t color the hen is — it's the [colo]r of the earlobe that determines [the] color of the egg."

"What color are yours Mom?"

"Hush now and go to sleep. I don't want to hear another peep out of any of you."

Big Jack and Goldie slept in late the next morning, but the peeps had been awake since the crack of dawn — waiting to go outside for a new adventure.

Finally Goldie and Big Jack made their way out into the morning sunshine.

The peeps were just chatterboxes.

"I liked the baby geese. Are we going to see the baby geese again today — Pop?"

"What are we going to see today Dad — more animals?"

"Bugs Bugs — yuk! What's this thing — a bird?"

[Wh]y do you [mean s]purs and mama [...]?"

"Didn't the birds & bees tell you anything?"

"Same as yesterday — bugs!"

"What's fer breakfast?"

"Why are these flowers blue and those other ones yellow?"

They showed the peeps the barn, the woodshed, the orchard and even the garden———— but they didn't want to show them off to any more of the animals. They didn't think they could stand more disappointment————

then Goldie came up with an idea.

"Big Jack——— I know who might like to see our peeps. The girls back at the henhouse."

"Yes, maybe you're right——— let's mozy over to the chicken yard."

Clara was the first to see them coming.

"Well, I declare — what a sight for sore eyes. Here comes Goldie and her new baby peeps."

"Hi Kids, I'm your Aunt Betty!"

"Oh, they're just precious. I could just kiss 'em!"

"Look girls, this is little Jack ain't he a chip off the ol'"

"Oh look girls, how cute! What's your name sugar?"

Proud wasn't the word for it... Big Jack was bustin' his buttons. He and Goldie were so glad that they had the girls' approval.

But Big Jack couldn't wait to show them Mr. Lowell's studio

And with that they went off for their next adventure.

"Now this is Mr. Lowell's studio———. Come on in, but wipe your feets———.
I want to show you all somethin'! You know, as I've told you,——— Mr. Lowell is
somewhat of a shade-tree painter———. Well this is sort of a museum———.
You might even call it the CHICKEN HALL OF FAME. I discovered it a long time
ago———.In fact, it was the day I stold your mother's heart——— Right Goldie?"

This is your Great Grandfather. Everyone called him Smilin' Jack. He came over from
the old country———.He was one of the first roosters Mr. Lowell had.
Little Jack, get back here———. I'm gonna give y'all a quiz after this.
And down here we have your Aunt Evelyn——— . . ."

This first room is kinda like a nursery —, with paintings of youngins here on the farm.

This is your Aunt Pearl. Mr. Lowell slipped a bunch of different types of eggs under her while she was setting on her nest. When they hatched they were all different colors.

But she raised and loved them as if they were her own."

"Who's that?"

" Well that's my baby picture — when I was only knee high to a grasshopper."

" The babies in these two paintings were hatched by what they call an incubator. Now, that means that a machine was the mother."

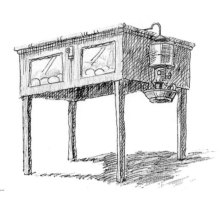

"As you may have heard, Mr. Lowell grew up in Red Oak, Missouri———— and the local farmers would bring their poultry into town to sell to his dad.

This painting shows how they were stored in crates at the side shed———— until the delivery truck would come by and get them ———— and take them to the big city of Carthage."

"The rest of these are just some more old chicken paintings————. But none of these are of me, so let's just go on over here..."

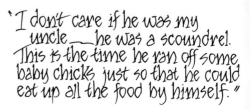

"I don't care if he was my uncle — he was a scoundrel. This is the time he ran off some baby chicks just so that he could eat up all the food by himself."

"Now that's your Great Uncle, Louie the Leghorn — he's on your mother's side of the family.

He thought he was the most handsome dude ever, and that all the hens on the farm should fall head over heels in love with him."

"Well, he always wanted to see the world — unfortunately, he got to."

"What ever happened to him?"

"Here are some ducks and geese in the north cornfield."

"Look gang! There's the roof of the old corncrib we were hatched under."

"Here's a couple of turkeys in the timber eating acorns. Hate 'em myself.— Guess it's whatever floats your boat."

"You can tell by the frost on the pumpkin that Thanksgiving is near—unknown by Mr. Tom."

"These strange lookin' critters are Guineas—none of which you would want to buy a used car from."

"Are they the ones that sound like an old gate that needs oilin'?"

"Yes, but— let's look at some paintings that are more pleasant."

"Well, after yesterday— geese aren't my favorite subject. But after all, they are distant relatives.."

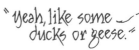

"Yeah, like some ducks or geese."

"Now this is a painting of Billy the Bantam as he was trying to make it back to the chicken house during a rainstorm and a gaggle of geese was givin' him a bad time."

"Oh look, how cute!"

"Yes, those are baby ducks

and their proud parents out on Uncle Remus' pond with an old bullfrog watchin'."

"This is a painting of Miss Charlotte gathering eggs.
     If Mr. Lowell gathers them he would just use his hat."

"And this is Mr. Lowell coming home from market."

I remember that day — April and Miss Charlotte was hanging up their wash when a sudden gust of wind blew a shirt off — and your Dad thought Willy had got him for sure _____."

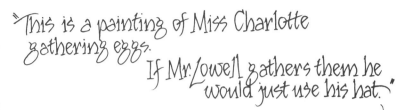

I really don't see the humor in that Goldie... Let's go on into the Hall of Horrors.

N ow in this room are some paintings of some real bad dudes. They sleep all day, then when the sun goes down and the moon comes up ___ all the critters you see here come out and head for the chicken house, in hopes that Mr. Lowell forgot to shut the door."

"This painting is called, 'When Shadows Come Alive'."

"Should I be skeered of shadows?"

"Yes, if you go outside after dark. ___ How many critters do you see in this painting?"

"This is old Mr. Owl. No matter how many times I hear him hoot it still makes the feathers on the back of my neck stand up."

Here are a couple of raccoons that are up to no good. If they aren't tryin' to get into the chicken house they are raidin' the corn crib.

Now, Mr. Red tailed Hawk is a daytime predator. Although the old-timers call him a chicken hawk ___ I've really never seen one try and get one on this farm ___ But I still don't trust him any further than I can throw Barney the Workhorse.

Now here is a critter you wouldn't want to come across on a dark night. It's Mr. Skunk lookin' into a brooder house where the farmer keeps his hens and chicks."

"Do he eat them up?"

"No — you see the farmer comes out and shuts the door for the night."

"This is Reynard the Fox makin' his nightly rounds — checkin' to make sure that the doors are all locked."

"This is a painting of ol' Brer Fox — when another farmer owned this farm — and left the hen house door un-locked one night.

This painting gives your Mom the willies."

"She calls this one... 'Justice!'"

"Speakin' of critters — it's getting dark. I think we had better start mozyin' back to the corncrib for the night."

It had been a long day and the sun was just setting

as Big Jack and Goldie along with their peeps left the studio

And to this day they are all real chickens living on a real farm —— here in Southwest Missouri.

Better hurry up lil Jack-a-pussom goin' get ya!

The end